:

LEGEND OF THE PINK DOLPHIN

TERRY KRASZEWSKI and

HEATHER DAWN KRASZEWSKI

ISBN: 9781729237304

Surf Angel Publications

To Audre, Amy and Adam,

DEDICATION

Surf Angel is dedicated to the angels in our lives who guide and inspire us, and the lovers of the ocean who respect and protect its beauty and wonder.

Reach for the stars!

3

CONTENTS

1 - *ENCHANTED EVENING*

The sun slowly sets on the calm waters of the ocean. Perched high above in the clouds is an angel. She watches contentedly as the pink and purple sunset fades to a dark blue night sky.

One by one, the stars begin to appear and she smiles. Dressed in a purple and white polka dot swimsuit, Surf Angel picks up her surfboard and is ready to embark on her nightly journey.

Light as a feather, she jumps on her board and magically glides down gossamer moonlit clouds to the vast blue water below. Surrounded by a shimmering glow, her lavender surfboard slows and levitates just above the ocean's surface.

Just below her, she sees colorful starfish and barnacles cling to a wet, sandy rock. Crabs click their claws in greeting to Surf Angel. She giggles and gently passes her hand over them, sprinkling magical sleep sparkles. The little crabs yawn, and crawl into their crannies to sleep.

In the distance, the rhythmic clang of a buoy is heard. Surf Angel summons a wave, and silently rides toward it.

A family of seals are perched on the large red buoy. Seeing Surf Angel, a baby seal swims out to meet her. He carries a squid in his mouth, and places it on the deck of her surfboard.

"For me?" she asks.

The baby seal nods excitedly.

"Thank you very much," she smiles, patting his head, "I know squid is your favorite. Are you sure you don't want to keep it for your bedtime snack?"

The little seal considers this; squids are his favorite and this one looks so juicy. He looks up at Surf Angel with conflicted eyes.

"I don't mind," she assures him, "I know how much you like them."

She places the squid in his open mouth and he eagerly chews it. Surf Angel laughs.

"Aw, see? It makes me happy to see you happy."

Together the baby seal and Surf Angel glide to the buoy. He leaps onto the metal ledge and scoots close to his mother. The mother seal drapes her flipper protectively across the baby, snuggling him.

Surf Angel lifts up her hand and showers the seal family in sparkles and they slowly, peacefully close their eyes.

"Thank you again," she whispers to the baby seal.

The little seal gives a contended sigh, and falls asleep.

Surf Angel continues to surf along on her magical board. The waves move her across the glassy sea. Next to her, a gigantic grey whale surfaces and blows a powerful spout of water. Surf Angel smiles and marvels at his enormity and grace.

Surf Angel lifts up her hand and blows sparkles from her palm. The whale smiles at her and submerges, waving his fluke 'goodnight'.

2 - *TROUBLE BELOW*

Sea turtles, starfish and seahorses have all been visited by Surf Angel. She skims along silently, surveying the quiet ocean.

As she surfs, a dorsal fin suddenly appears in the wave beside her. Surf Angel kicks out of the wave to see who it is: a dolphin.

Surf Angel lays on the surfboard on her tummy and gently pets the dolphin.

"Hello there, my friend. Why aren't you sleeping?"

The dolphin looks at her with worried eyes, and chatters at her with anxious pops and clicks.

Surf Angel listens to her with concern.

"Oh my goodness. There is no time to waste. Take me there!" she urges.

The dolphin dives underwater and swims away

at high speed.

Surf Angel catches a wave and swiftly follows her.

Soon, the dolphin stops, pops up, and frantically chatters. Surf Angel paddles over to her and slides off her board to peer under the water.

Surf Angel and the dolphin dive down to find a young dolphin caught in a fishing net. There is something unusual about this baby. She is not grey but very pink in color.

Under the water, the dolphin dad is trying desperately to free the baby struggling against its bonds. The little dolphin baby is entwined and tangled. It is very weak and can barely get to the surface to breathe.

Surf Angel gently places her glowing hands around the frightened dolphin's head.

"Be calm, little one. I will set you free."

The tiny dolphin relaxes as Surf Angel carefully untwists the fishing net that is restricting her.

Little by little, the ropes loosen and the baby is set free.

The young dolphin is exhausted and injured from

her ordeal. Her strength gone, she begins to sink.

Surf Angel and the dolphin parents together quickly push her up and help her to stay on the water's surface.

The baby dolphin relieved, takes a big deep breath of air.

"Poor, darling." Surf Angel sighs.

She looks up to the sky and sees that the night is paling. She realizes it will soon be morning.

Surf Angel must return to the heavens above before sunrise. She tells the dolphin parents,

"She needs time to rest. I know a cove where she'll be safe. May I take her there?"

The dolphin parents nod in agreement. Together they push the baby onto her surfboard.

Surf Angel briskly stands up on her board, closes her eyes and speaks these enchanting words:

"Sea fans sway to and fro, surround my surfboard in a starry glow."

Sparkles and an iridescent glow swirl around Surf Angel, the baby dolphin and her surfboard.

Her surfboard rises and begins to move forward, sailing across the water at a high rate of speed.

In no time at all, they slide into a quiet peaceful cove.

Carefully, Surf Angel places the baby dolphin on a smooth, submerged rock.

"Rest here, little one. Caring hearts and healing hands are on their way. I will be back to see you again at nightfall."

Surf Angel hugs the baby dolphin and softly kisses her nose. The baby dolphin weakly squeaks and nods. She completely trusts Surf Angel.

Surf Angel climbs on her surfboard and slowly flaps her wings.

The water beneath her board begins to rise, and a path of sparkles trail behind her board as she swiftly surfs up and away to the clouds above.

3 - *SANDCASTLE MORNING*

It's a beautiful morning at the beach. Kara and her brother Sean are busy putting the final touches on their project.

Kara is skillfully building a drip sand castle. Sean assists and carries over a bucket of water and wet sand.

"Ta-da!" Kara announces proudly, "Seven towers!"

"Seven? Why seven?" Sean asks.

"Because I'm seven years old, silly!" she smiles.

"So because I'm twelve, I'm supposed to drip twelve towers?! Forget that!" Sean scoffs, "Seven's the limit."

Kara dips her hand into the bucket to grab some sand and lets out a scream.

She drops the handful of sand, and a crustacean

scrambles away.

"It's just a sandcrab," Sean laughs, "It won't hurt you. You don't have to be scared."

"I wasn't scared! It tickled."

"You scream when you're tickled?"

Kara sticks her tongue out at him. Sean reaches out, and tickles Kara's sides.

"Ahhh! Stop it!" Kara giggles. Sean stops and they both laugh.

They stand back to admire their sand castle.

"I gotta admit it's a good one," Sean observes.

"Best one so far," Kara agrees, "Mom and Dad should see it."

"They're too busy working," Sean retorts, "you know that."

He picks up a stone and throws it in the water.

Kara sighs and snaps a photo of the castle with her camera.

Sand castle completed, Sean and Kara walk

along the water's edge, dodging waves.

Kara jumps over a clump of seaweed. Sean picks it up and drapes it across his shoulders.

"What are you doing, Sean?"

"I'm not Sean. I'm a sea monster! Rawr!"

Kara pretends to shriek and runs away. Sean chases her down the beach. They run faster and faster, in and out of the water following the rushing shoreline.

They reach the cove and carefully climb the slippery rocks that protect a small lagoon.

"Wait. Listen," Sean pauses when he hears a strange noise, "Do you hear that?"

They listen and hear a faint squeaking sound. Sean and Kara quietly and cautiously go inside the cove to investigate.

The sound is getting louder.

Peering from behind a rock, they discover what is making the sound. They see a baby dolphin partially submerged and nestled on a rocky ledge.

"Whoa!" Sean exclaims, "It's a dolphin!"

"A baby dolphin," Kara corrects, "Sean, it's pink!"

"It sure is!" Sean agrees.

Excited, Kara takes the camera out of her pocket and snaps a photo. Sean rolls his eyes.

"I have to get a picture!" she insists, "Who is ever going to believe we saw a pink dolphin?"

Sean sighs, "You've got a point there."

The baby dolphin squeaks louder, with fear.

Moving closer, Sean notices there are lacerations on the dolphin's skin.

Crouching down, Sean inspects more closely, "She doesn't look too good. Her breathing is unsteady and look at all the cuts on her skin. She's hurt."

"She needs help!" Kara jumps up and grabs Sean's arm and tries to drag him away.

"Come on, Sean!" she urges, "Let's go get Mom and Dad! Hurry!"

"Okay, okay," Sean says and quickly follows her.

4 - *HELP IS ON THE WAY*

Kara bursts into the Sealife Sanctuary, not far from the cove. A volunteer is feeding lettuce to an injured turtle.

"Hi! Where's Mom and Dad?" Kara asks as Sean trails behind her.

"In the exam room giving the walrus a check-up."

"Thanks!" Kara rushes off.

"Hey, no running!"

Dad and another volunteer gently reassure the walrus as Mom listens to his heart with her stethoscope.

"Sounds good," she nods, "he's got a good, strong heartbeat."

The walrus burps loudly.

"Oh, and even stronger breath." Dad groans, waving away the smell.

Mom stands, patting him gently as they release the walrus, "Off you go, handsome."

The walrus sits up and then lumbers slowly back into his pool.

"Well, what do you think?" asks Dad.

"He's great. One hundred percent," she smiles, "Six months of tender loving care and we can now return him to the wild."

"Six months of tender loving care and one hundred fifty-five pounds of clams and sea cucumbers a day. I'll miss him, but I won't miss his food bill." Dad nods.

"Mom! Dad!" Kara shouts.

"What is it, Kara?" asks Mom.

"We saw a dolphin," Kara exclaims, trying to catch her breath.

Their parents relax, and go back to their clean-up work, "That's nice. Did you see a pod swim by?"

"No, actually we found it in the cove and

it's hurt," Sean explains, "you need to come and check it out."

Mom is instantly concerned, "Ok, let me get my bag and you can take me where you found him."

Dad sighs, "We just finished with the walrus -"

"It's not a him," Kara corrects as she and Mom head for the door, "it's a girl."

"What makes you so sure?" asks Mom.

"She's pink!"

Mom and Dad look at each other, puzzled.

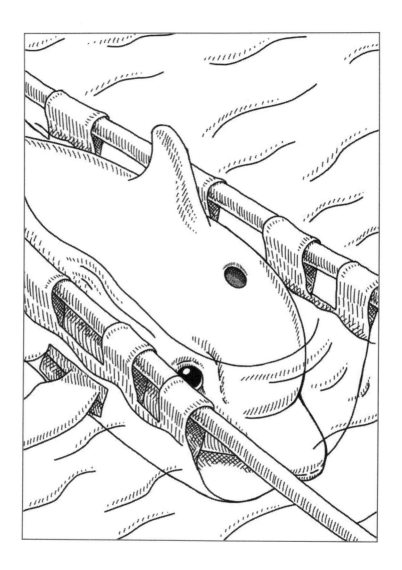

5 - *TRY IT, YOU'LL LIKE IT*

Hours later, the pink dolphin is suspended in a holding tank. Laying in a sling, it will keep her afloat and her breathing hole above water.

"Is she gonna be ok?" asks Kara.

"I think so," Mom nods, "she's very weak. Her wounds need to be treated. She needs food and antibiotics for those cuts. It's a good thing you found her when you did."

Dad crushes medicine, and puts it inside a fish. He hands it to Kara, "Maybe she'll take it from you."

"Eww! It's all slimy!" Kara complains.

"She'll love it though," Dad smiles.

Kara leans over the rail to reach the baby dolphin, "I have a delicious fish for you."

The little dolphin shies away.

"I know. I don't think it looks very good either but my dad says you'll like it."

The dolphin unhappily squeaks, rejecting the fish.

"Darn it. She won't take it," Kara frowns.

"That's alright," Mom assures, "we'll give her nutrients through a feeding tube until she feels like eating on her own."

Mom leaves to prepare the medicine.

Kara gently rubs the dolphin's head, "Don't worry - Mom's going to fix you up in no time."

Show and Tell

6 - *SHOW AND TELL*

Kara sits at her school desk and waits impatiently as a boy finishes his Show and Tell presentation.

"And that's how I got this pencil-topper and met a fireman!"

He bows and the class applauds.

"Thank you, Lance," the teacher says, "An intriguing story but I would like to remind everyone that shoving any body part inside the prize machine at the arcade is never a good idea. I'm very glad Fireman Jones was able to free your arm without injury."

Lance grins, and sits down as Kara raises her hand.

"I'm sure your parents are very proud," the teacher smiles and nods, "Kara, you're up."

Kara stands in front of the class.

"Not long ago, my family rescued a baby dolphin. She was hurt, and we've been helping her get better. We feed her fish and medicine and give her lots of love. She's doing better, and when she's all healed, she'll go back to the ocean. I brought pictures."

Kara holds up a handful of photos and the children scoot closer to see.

"Something's wrong with your camera," one of the boys complains, "She looks pink."

"She is pink," Kara corrects.

"No way!" a boy shouts.

"Uh huh," Kara confirms.

"Whoa!"

"I wanna go see her for real!" a girl exclaims.

"Me too!"

"Field trip! Field trip! Field trip!" the class begins to chant.

7 - *FIELD TRIP*

The class and chaperones gather around the tank to see the little dolphin.

"Welcome," Mom smiles, "I'm so glad you could be here today and meet our newest guest.

She is a bottlenose dolphin. Bottlenose dolphins are mammals, which means they drink milk from their mothers and are warm-blooded.

To keep their temperature up, they are surrounded by a thick layer of fat called 'blubber' just below the skin.

They can stay underwater and hold their breath up to fifteen minutes.

They breathe oxygen, just like us, so they need quick access to air. Usually, bottlenose dolphins are shallow divers and stay close to the surface.

To find food and navigate, they use

echolocation. This is performed by sending ultrasound

through the water which is bounced back to the dolphin. Are there any questions?"

The kids raise their hands.

"Why is she pink?" a little girl asks intently.

"We're not quite sure," Mom answers, "We just know she's very special. I know I have never seen one before."

Another child raises their hand, "Does she have a name?"

"Yes, she does!" Kara blurts out, "Her name is Coral!"

"There you have it." Mom nods, "It suits her."

Dad smiles and motions to the kids, "Okay children, Coral needs quiet time, so everyone follow me. Let's go visit the turtles."

"Cool! BYE, CORAL!"

As the group is shuffled off to the next room, the teacher pulls Mom aside.

"Thank you for allowing us to visit today. The children are really thrilled to be here."

"Of course. We love to share and educate," Mom smiles.

"It's my understanding that your facility runs primarily on donations?"

"Yes, it's true," Mom nods, "All of our staff are volunteers and work without pay. They really are committed, and believe very much in what we do here."

"Well then, please accept this gift. This is for the animals." the teacher hands Mom an envelope.

"What's this?"

"The parents and the children really would like to help."

The plump envelope has money in it.

"Oh, my. This is unexpected. Thank you SO much!"

"We had plans to visit the local bread factory. They were charging ten dollars per child. We all decided giving you the money was something we could all feel good about."

"Well, thank you," Mom smiles, "Coral has her appetite back and this will buy a lot of fish."

"Do you mind if I post the video I just took of Coral online?" the teacher asks.

"No, we don't mind." Mom assures, "Everyone should know about this special little dolphin."

8 - *HELPING HANDS*

Dad and Sean pull up to the facility in their pickup truck, filled with crates of fish.

A TV News van is parked outside. A man with perfectly combed hair, wearing a crisp blue blazer approaches Dad.

"Sir, is it true that you have a pink dolphin here?" the man asks.

"Yes, we are caring for an injured dolphin that happens to be pink," Dad answers.

"Will you give us permission to film it?"

"Are you a reporter?" Sean asks.

"Technically, I'm a news station production assistant," the man concedes.

"What does that mean?" Sean wonders.

"Right now, I drive the equipment van and

chauffer our cameraman."

The cameraman gives a dignified nod.

"Then why are you all dressed up?" Sean quizzes.

"Dress for the job you want, not the one you have," the man smiled, "And I really want to be an on-air reporter. My niece was here recently on a field trip and sent me the little video her teacher shot. I think it would make a great story. Could we come inside? Do an interview...see the pink dolphin?"

"Sure, I don't see why not," Dad shrugs.

"Could you help us carry in the fish?" Sean asks.

The man and burly cameraman laugh. Dad and Sean wait.

"Oh," the man stammers, "you're serious?"

"We'd appreciate the help," Dad nods.

Dad, Sean, and crew begin grabbing boxes of fish.

Kara opens the back door for them.

"We've got some volunteers!" Dad smiles to her.

"We're actually here to do a news segment about your dolphin," the man explains, "Coral's an internet sensation! It's gotten one hundred thousand views in just twenty-four hours!"

Kara gasps in excitement, "Really?! Wow!"

"Darn right, wow!" the man boasts, "This story's going on my reel, they're bound to make me a reporter with this!"

9 - *MAKING HEADLINES*

The next morning, Kara accompanies her Mom on her daily rounds at the center.

"Coral looked so pretty on TV!" Kara smiles.

"She did," Mom agrees holding a stack of papers, "Would you help me get these charts filed away?"

Kara and Mom walk into the office and hear the voicemail beeping.

"The message light is on," Kara informs and pushes the play button.

"You have twenty-two messages." the machine announces.

Kara and Mom look at each other shocked.

"Hello, Marge Gimball from the Daily News. I was told you are caring for a pink dolphin. I would love to do a story about it. Please call me back.

Thank you."

Beep!

"Hi, Frank Harold, Wake Up Weekly. Our morning show would like to air a piece on your pink dolphin. Give me a call so we can set up a filming schedule. Thanks."

Beep!

On and on the messages played. Newspapers, magazines, TV shows, all wanting to see Coral.

"Wow! Coral's famous!" Kara beams.

Dad comes into the office, "You won't believe what's going on outside. Check it out!"

Kara, Mom and Dad pull open the curtain and see a crowd of people gathered outside by the gate.

"What do you think they want?" Mom asks.

"To see Coral!" Dad and Kara answer.

10 - *SURPRISE VISITOR*

It's nighttime. Kara and Dad are still at the office.

Kara works on her homework as her Dad combs through a large pile of paperwork.

"How's it going over there?" he asks.

"Good," Kara nods, "I have to circle the verbs in each sentence. A verb is a word that shows action."

"Correct," Dad smiles, "did you find them all?"

"I think so," she reads from the page, "'Sharks swim quickly.' Swim is the verb."

"Very nice," Dad smiles approvingly.

Homework completed, Kara puts her worksheet in her backpack, "How about you, Dad? Are you done with your homework yet?"

"Not yet," he sighs, "Still going through the

bills."

"There sure are a lot of them," Kara notices.

"Well, kiddo, it takes a lot to keep this place running. We have to pay for the utilities, food and the medicine for the animals. Oh, and rent on the building. The usual... but nothing you need to worry about," he smiles weakly, "If you're all finished, you can go check on Coral before we go. I'm sure she'd love to see you."

"Okay!" Kara smiles.

Kara sits on the edge of Coral's tank and strokes her snout.

"I thought you'd like to know that everyone in town saw you on the news and now they want to see you in person. Coral, YOU are a sensation."

Coral squeaks in reply.

"Right," Kara nods, "but crowds of people cause too much excitement for you. Mom says that you are not to be disturbed. You need time to rest and heal."

Coral squirts water from her blowhole.

"Hey, careful," Kara laughs, "You'll get me

wet!"

A tiny giggle is heard behind her.

Kara turns and sees Surf Angel.

"Hello," she smiles, "I'm Surf Angel. It's nice to see you again, Kara."

Kara stares at Surf Angel hovering above Coral's tank. Surf Angel lovingly pats Coral.

"How do you know my name?" Kara asks, astonished.

"I keep watch over children and seababies all over the world to make sure they are safe. That includes you and our little pink friend."

Coral squeaks in delight.

"She's very special, isn't she?" Kara says.

Surf Angel explains, "A pink dolphin is extremely rare. The legend tells us only one is born every one hundred years. She is a symbol of joy and love. A gift to the world.

All the sea animals know this. Now I am sharing this secret with you. I know you understand how important it is to watch over her and to return her to her family."

"We've been taking care of Coral," Kara says, "She's beginning to eat on her own now! As soon as she's healthy, my family will return her to the sea."

"I know." Surf Angel nods, "That is why I placed her where I knew you and your brother would find her. You have a beautiful heart, Kara. You've been doing a wonderful job. This separation has been very difficult for her parents. They miss her terribly."

"Coral's Mom and Dad?"

"Yes. I give them a report about her every night, so they won't worry."

"Every night?" Kara wonders.

"I have visited Coral every night since she was brought here. You are usually at home in bed at this hour."

Kara blushes, "I know. I was keeping my dad company."

Surf Angel gives Coral a kiss on the nose.

"I see. Well, it's time for me to go and take care

of my nightly duties."

"Duties?" Kara asks.

"Yes, visiting the creatures and wonders of the sea."

Surf Angel's surfboard suddenly appears and hovers in the air.

"Whoa," Kara whispers, "that is so cool! Do you fly or surf on that?!"

"I do a little of both. I surf the ocean and the airwaves. How would you like to come along with me tonight?" Surf Angel invites.

"Me? Really? YES! Of course!"

Surf Angel smiles.

"Oh, but my Dad..."

Surf Angel closes her eyes, "I see him. He works so hard and is very tired. He has alot of responsibility."

"He'll worry about where I am." Kara considers.

Surf Angel presses her hands together, "Heavy eyelids, stressful mind. Rest now and visit dreams that are kind."

Surf Angel opens her eyes, "There now. Your father can take a little rest while we're gone."

Surf Angel climbs onto her surfboard, and flaps her beautiful iridescent wings. Magical sparkles rain down upon Kara.

Smiling and in awe, Kara holds Surf Angel's hand and steps up onto the shiny purple long board.

Kara realizes the surfboard is surprisingly firm and stable. Clouds begin to billow from underneath and propel them up and up into the sky.

Clouds and wind rush past, Surf Angel and Kara look down upon the moonlit ocean below.

Soaring through the sky, they descend down to the water and skim along the surface.

"Not all forests are on land," Surf Angel waves her hand and gently cascades illuminating sparkles on the submerged canopy, "Kelp forests provide food and shelter for thousands of species. The forest grows taller every day, using sunlight from the sky and nutrients from the water."

A blade of kelp moves and an otter emerges.

"Otters love to explore and search out yummy things to eat. Clams, sea cucumbers and urchins are some of the food they might find."

Kara smiles as the otter lies on his back and places his food on his furry tummy.

Otter begins munching on his chewy cucumber.

Small bubbles pop to the surface and a green sea turtle floats up. He is chewing on a piece of seaweed.

"Green sea turtles can be underwater for hours at a time. They sleep just below the surface, under rocks and ledges."

Turtle winks at Surf Angel and slowly sinks under the water.

Having finished his snack, otter uses his paws to clean his face. He grabs a large kelp leaf and rolls.

Kara giggles.

"Tucking himself in," Surf Angel nods, "Otters roll in kelp so they won't drift away while sleeping."

They catch a curling wave and glide briskly across the ocean. Kara puts out her arms and leans with the motion of the board.

Splash!

Kara and Surf Angel dodge and are nearly doused by water. Loud slaps are heard hitting the ocean's surface.

"What was that?!" Kara whispers nervously.

"Manta rays," Surf Angel answers, "You don't need to worry, they're only interested in plankton and very small fish."

"Why are they jumping?" Kara wonders.

Surf Angel smiles, "Some say it's to get a better view of their prey," shakes her head, "but right now it's a game of showing off to see who can jump the highest and get the biggest splash."

Surf Angel waves her hand, scattering sparkles onto the rambunctious rays.

They stretch their fin wings and drift slowly down to the coral reef below to sleep.

Though Kara has lived and played at the ocean her entire life, she has never experienced it in this way.

She always considered animals precious but seeing them by the side of Surf Angel, it deepened her appreciation for their individual uniqueness and ability to cohabitate in an ocean they call home.

Arriving back at the center, Surf Angel guides the surfboard to Coral's tank and helps Kara step down to the ground once again.

"It's almost sunrise. Time to be on my way. I will see you again soon, Kara," Surf Angel smiles, drifting up. Surf Angel guides her sparkly surfboard upward. She blows Kara a kiss and flies away into the dawning morning.

Kara nods and waves goodbye. She stretches out her arms, looking at her own glittering skin. She smiles broadly, shaking her head in wonder.

Going back to the office, Kara sees her Dad still sound asleep at his desk.

Kara touches Dad's shoulder, "Dad, wake up. It's time to go home."

58

11 - *LET'S MAKE A DEAL*

Dad is in the food preparation area, chopping vegetables.

"I'm sorry but that's not the way it works here," Mom says as Kara and Sean follow her and a visitor.

Dad pauses his task and looks up to observe a large man in an expensive suit and flashy jewelry speaking to Mom.

"Preposterous, everything is negotiable," the man says.

Dad begins to say "Hello," but is abruptly interrupted.

Thrusting his hand out to shake, "Good morning, sir. I am Morton McLavish. Investor and entrepreneur extraordinaire."

"Nice to meet you." nods Dad.

"Mister McLavish-" Mom sighs.

"Please, my friends call me Morton." he smiles.

"Mister McLavish," Mom continues explaining to Dad, "says he would like to purchase our animals."

"For how much?" Sean asks.

"What?" asks Dad, confused.

"No, no, no," Mister McLavish shakes his head, "You misunderstand. I don't want to buy your animals. That's just silly."

"Oh, well then." Dad says.

"I only want to buy the pink dolphin."

"What? NO!" Kara shouts.

"It's alright, Kara." Mom assures her.

"It's not alright!" Kara protests, "He can't have Coral!"

"I'm sorry, sir," Mom tells him, "But none of the animals here are for sale. We are a rehabilitation center. The animals we care for are released back into the wild once they are recovered and healthy."

"How noble." Mister McLavish scoffs, "Tell me

how do you keep up with expenses? Food, medicine, the people to care for the animals. It all costs money."

"Our center is run by donations and volunteers." Dad answers.

"Heartwarming," Mister McLavish nods, "I admire your work. I really do.

If I had the time, I might take off my diamond cufflinks, roll up my silk sleeves and toss sardines to these amazing amphibians."

"Actually," Sean squints, "they're not-"

"But I don't have a lot of time," Mister McLavish interrupts, "What I do have is a lot of money. I simply must have that marvelous pink dolphin."

"Well, you can't have her!" Kara insists.

"Do you own the dolphin?" he skeptically asks Kara.

"No one owns her!" Kara informs him, "She's going back to her family in the ocean once she's well."

"But what if I can offer her a better life?" Mister McLavish queries, "One filled with fame and legions of fans?"

"Huh?" Kara wonders.

Mister McLavish produces a large scroll of building plans and theatrically unfurls it.

"Behold! This is FantaSEA! An amazing aquatic candy-colored wonderland!"

"Are those waterslides?" asks Sean.

"Yes!" Mister McLavish beams, "I'm building a brand new resort in Atlantic City, and I want it all to be centered around the world's only pink dolphin! She will be my star. A pink glittery water stadium created just for her. Three shows a day, seven days a week. I'll hire top trainers to teach her tricks. We'll produce special Coral merchandise. Imagine it. People will flock from all around the globe to see her!"

Kara glares at Mister McLavish, crossing her arms unmoved by his presentation, "Coral is not for sale."

"Everything has a price," Mister McLavish shrugs and hands Dad a business card, "Give me a call when you decide on yours."

He leaves in a huff. Sean closes the door and turns to the family.

"Are you kidding me?!" he shouts, "A guy walks in and offers us cash, and you say 'No'? End of discussion?!"

"Sean, he wanted to buy Coral. We don't own her," Mom shakes her head, "You know that's not what we do here."

"Right," Sean nods, "What we do is work our shriveled, water-logged fingers to the bone every single day, and spend all of our money on fish. Do you know how it feels to walk around town smelling like a sardine?!"

Dad reasons, "Your mother and I chose to dedicate our lives to helping animals that are in need -"

"Jeez!" Sean groans, "Give me his phone number. I'll paint myself pink, and maybe he'll buy me!"

"Don't go, Sean!" Kara says, throwing her arms around him, "I love you!"

Sean rolls his eyes and sighs as Kara clings to him.

12 - *FOR GOOD MEASURE*

Kara and Sean sit on the dock outside of the Sealife Sanctuary. Sean holds a bucket, and playfully tosses small fish one-by-one to a pelican. The pelican catches it easily in his large pouch and swallows the fish whole.

"Good catch!" Kara winces, wiping off the splatter.

"That's how he likes it," Sean shrugs, "Fresh and juicy!"

"Do you know how much water he can hold in his bill?" Kara quizzes.

"How much?"

"Three gallons!" she exclaims. "That's a lot," Sean concedes.

In the distance, they see a man pushing a metal rod with a wheel attached to the end. As they watch, he rolls it while walking around the perimeter of their building.

"That's weird. What is that thing?" Kara wonders.

"I don't know." Sean replies.

Sean stands up and shouts to the man, "Excuse me? What'cha doing?"

The man stops and smiles, "Oh, just taking a little stroll around the property."

He pushes a button, and continues pushing the wheeled rod to the end of the building. He then puts the equipment into his car and drives away.

Sean hands Kara the last fish, "Here. Last one."

"Ewww!" she complains, taking it as Sean runs inside to find his parents.

Kara places the fish on the rail next to the pelican. The pelican scoops it up and gulps it down happily.

Sean and Mom come outside.

"Do you know what he wanted?" Mom asks Kara.

"I don't know," Kara says, wiping her hands on her shorts, "But he had a metal stick with a wheel on it and it made a clicking noise when he moved it."

Mom shakes her head, "Hmmm, sounds like it was a rolling tape measure."

"What are those for?" Sean asks.

"Measuring. Nothing for you to worry about," Mom sighs and goes back inside.

13 - *IT'S JUST BUSINESS*

Kara and Sean walk into the Rehabilitation Center after school.

"And then the seahorses do a dance!" Kara informs.

"A dance?" Sean wonders.

"Yeah, kind of a twirling, floating dance!" Kara begins to demonstrate.

Sean shakes his head, "You're a natural. Are you sure you're not part seahorse?"

"I wish!" she shouts.

Sean shushes her, listening.

"What?" she whispers.

"Come on," Sean motions for her to follow him.

They hear a loud conversation taking place in the

office. The kids sneak closer to listen, and stand behind the open door.

They hear Mom talking to the owner of the building and Mister McLavish.

Mom says, "But we have been your tenant for ten years -"

"Ten underpaid years," McLavish interrupts, "a property such as this should be going for double the amount that he has been charging you. I had my man measure the footage."

"So you're the reason that man was measuring the building," Mom glares.

"Of course," McLavish nods, "I wanted to make an informed offer."

"Look," the landlord explains, "we have operated on a month-to-month lease and I'd like to think I've been understanding when your payment has been late."

"Yes," Dad agrees, "you have been -"

"But you are two months behind on the rent, and Mister McLavish is expressing interest in taking over the lease and paying more."

"And on time!" McLavish adds.

"But you know our situation," Mom reasons, "we always pay when we have the money, it's just -"

"Listen: Mister McLavish's offer is just too good to pass up. If you can match his offer, you can stay. Otherwise, he will be the new tenant of this property and you will have to leave. I'm truly sorry."

The landlord quickly leaves the office. Kara and Sean stay behind the door.

McLavish smiles, "Finally, a reasonable person."

"Double the rent?" Mom glares, "What kind of a man -"

"The kind that gets what he wants, madam!" McLavish retorts, "Now I can solve this problem, and solve it very easily. I am offering to give you the equivalent of a full year's rent plus a hefty sum... as a tax-deductible donation, of course."

Dad and Mom stare at him, quizzically.

"All I ask in return is the small, adorable pink dolphin."

"No!" Kara shouts as Sean covers her mouth.

Dad and Mom look at each other, contemplating. They sigh and nod.

Dad slowly stands up from behind his desk. McLavish stands and offers his hand to shake on it.

Instead of shaking hands, Dad angrily points to the door, "I'm asking you to leave! This is still our center, and you are not welcome here."

"For the time being," McLavish exhales sharply, straightening his cuffs, "I will see you in thirty days."

"Get out now!" Dad loudly repeats.

McLavish marches out and grumbles to himself, "SO rude. It's nothing personal. It's just business. Why don't they get that?"

Strutting back to his limousine, McLavish fusses and straightens his cuffs and jacket. Perched high on the roof of the sanctuary, the pelican spies something interesting and sparkly on the wrist of the man walking below. Swooshing down with beak poised for the catch, the pelican swoops and grabs at McLavish's dazzling diamond cufflink. Startled by the aerial attack, McLavish instantly protects his perfectly combed hair. On target, the pelican plucks and snatches the glittery jewel and victoriously flies away with his prize securely in his pouch.

"What? My diamond! I have been robbed and assaulted by a flying pickpocket!"

Watching the pelican fly away towards the beach, McLavish realizes his cufflink is gone forever.

Fists raised to the sky, he shouts, "When I take over, you'll be the first to go!"

Getting into his car, he shouts, "Driver, get me out of this zoo!"

Back in the center, Kara and Sean come out of hiding after McLavish leaves the building.

Kara is relieved, "Yes! Coral is safe."

"Coral? All you can think about is Coral?" Sean roars, "If we sold her, we would have so much money! Just imagine, we could buy anything we want! Think about it! Mom and Dad wouldn't have to work so hard and worry all the time."

"Sean, Coral is not our's to sell," Kara insists, "she belongs to the sea. Her parents are waiting for her. Surf Angel told me herself."

"Surf Angel?" Sean asks, "Who's the Surf

Angel?"

"She watches over the creatures of the sea. She visits Coral every night."

"Of course, she does," Sean scoffs, "And you know this because?"

"We're friends! I even flew with her on her magical surfboard," Kara informs, matter-of-factly, moving her arms like she's surfing. "At first, I thought it was a dream. But look, I still have some sparkle left!"

"Ok, now I know we really need the money because you need to see a psychiatrist."

Kara glares at Sean, "I don't care if you believe me or not. Coral is going to get better, and then she's going home to the ocean to be with her parents. That's where she belongs, not with that crumby, rotten Mister McLavish!"

14 - *WHEN LIFE GIVES YOU LEMONS*

"Sean? Sean!" Kara shouts, "Hurry up! Help me!"

Sean rushes to the front door and finds Kara tottering into the house with a bulging backpack and a full grocery bag hanging on each arm.

"Oh, thanks. They are really heavy!" she complains.

Sean takes the bags, and helps her take off the backpack. It drops to the floor with a loud "Thud!".

"Jeez, what do you have in there? Rocks?"

"No," Kara unzips the pack, "lemons!"

"Lemons?" Sean asks.

"Yep," Kara smiles, "I picked as many lemons

as I could reach from our tree."

"Why?"

"So we can make lemonade! Sean, I have a brilliant idea! We are going to sell lemonade and use the money to save the center."

Sean rolls his eyes.

"Why do you always do that?" Kara asks.

"There is no way you're going to raise enough money selling lemonade."

"Not with that attitude," she considers, "Okay, you may have a point. What if we sell cookies too?"

Sean shakes his head, "Thirty days. The landlord gave Mom and Dad thirty days to come up with double the amount they usually pay. They could barely pay it as it was."

"But we can try, Sean. We have to try!"

"It's impossible." he insists.

Kara smiles.

"Why are you smiling?" Sean asks, irritated.

"If you met Surf Angel, you'd know that nothing is impossible."

"Not this again," he groans, "Did one of those lemons hit you in the head?"

"She's real," Kara assures him, "And if she's real, magic is real and that means anything is possible."

Sean sighs as he walks away, "I'm seriously worried that you have completely lost your mind."

"Oh! What if it's pink lemonade? Like Coral?" she gasps, "How do I make it pink?"

Kara begins to drag her full backpack into the kitchen.

"Come on, Sean. I need help making the

lemonade. Oh, and can you video me making it? We need to put it online! Sean?"

15 - *TEAMWORK MAKES THE DREAM WORK*

McLavish rides in the back of his limousine on his way to the Sealife Sanctuary. He speaks loudly into the phone.

"Yes, thirty days have come and gone. Time certainly does fly when you're creating an entertainment extravaganza for an aquatic superstar," he laughs, "The blueprints for the performing tank look fantastic. What's the progress on construction? Half way completed? Excellent!"

"Oh! And what about that lab technician? Pink dolphin DNA ought to bring a pretty penny. We need to get those samples right away so we can produce more of those pink wonders!" McLavish admires his diamond pinky ring as he listens, "Of course, it can be done! Haven't you heard of Jurassic Park? Idiot!"

McLavish realizes the limousine is not moving.

"Driver!" McLavish bellows,

"Why have we slowed down?"

"Traffic, sir."

"I'll have to call you back." McLavish hangs up the phone.

"I have a meeting to get to at that silly Sealife Sanctuary," McLavish grumbles.

"Sir, we've arrived at the Sanctuary but there's a large crowd filling the parking lot."

McLavish rolls down his window, and sees hundreds of people surrounding the rehab center.

"Just pull over," McLavish orders.

Confused, he gets out and begins walking towards the front of the crowd.

He pushes his way through the throngs of people. Finally, he sees the family with the landlord, speaking to a Television News reporter with perfectly combed hair, wearing his crisp blue blazer.

"It's the little Rehab Center that could," the reporter announces, "This ocean loving family and dedicated volunteers have been caring for injured animals for over a decade. Coral, the little pink dolphin, was recently rescued by these dedicated caregivers.

As a matter of fact, you might have seen my story on this remarkable little mammal in my television debut."

In the audience, heads nod in acknowledgement.

"Sadly, hard times have fallen on the center due to a drastic increase in rent. Now the Sanctuary finds itself in jeopardy of losing everything and closing their doors forever.

Well, that's when Kara, the young daughter of the center's founders, decided to take matters in hand. She came up with the grand idea to sell pink lemonade."

"And dolphin shaped cookies," Kara adds proudly, "my brother Sean helped me decorate them!"

"Pink lemonade and dolphin shaped cookies," the reporter nods, "to raise funds to save this Center. Word spread quickly about their cause and touched the hearts of people all over the world. From Tokyo to Timbuktu, children sent their pennies earned from the sales of their own lemonade stands. Men, women, and children mailed donations to this Rehab Center in hopes that it would help to keep its doors open. It seems everyone wants to help Coral get well and to ensure that Sealife Sanctuary will be here for other injured animals that may need help in the future."

McLavish looks warily around at the enthusiastic crowd. He watches and listens as the reporter hands his microphone over to Dad.

"We want to thank everyone here today and to all those who have given their support to our center. We are overwhelmed by your kindness and generosity. I have an exciting announcement to make. It is with great pleasure, I am here today to tell you all, that not only do we have enough money to pay the back rent, but now we can afford to buy the property outright!"

The crowd breaks out into loud approving cheers.

"So, to be clear, Sealife Sanctuary has been saved?" the reporter asked, excitedly.

"Yes, that is a fact," Dad nods, "Thanks to a little pink dolphin who inspired people to pitch in, work hard, and make a difference."

McLavish, hearing this announcement, slumps, his mouth agape.

Shocked, he watches as the landlord shakes Dad's hand, and triumphantly hands him the deed to the building.

McLavish, enraged, runs up and grabs the landlord's arm, "What is this double-cross? You never said this property was for sale!"

"Mister McLavish, everything has a price," the landlord retorts as he shrugs out of McLavish's grasp and walks away. "It's nothing personal."

"So tell us, what is Coral's future?" the reporter asks Dad.

"Coral's future is very bright," Dad smiles, "In fact, she just passed her physical exam. Tomorrow, we are happy to report we will release her back to the ocean where she belongs."

Hearing this good news, the crowd loudly cheers. McLavish furious, storms off making his way back to his car.

As he climbs into his limo, the phone rings.

"Yes, I saw the news report! I'm here, you idiot!"

he shouts, "No, I don't want you to stop construction! You worry about your crew, and let me worry about the dolphin!"

McLavish slams down the phone.

Muttering to himself, "Stupid kelp huggers. I am building a five star resort featuring the world's only pink dolphin. And a pink dolphin I shall have!"

"Driver, put a call through to the captain of my yacht. It's a time to implement my backup plan."

16 - *THIEF IN THE NIGHT*

It's nighttime and the crowds have all gone home. Sean walks through the darkened halls to have a last visit with Coral and to say goodbye to her.

Sean reaches the back area, flips on the lights and walks to Coral's tank.

"Coral?" he calls, holding a bucket of fish, "Come on, Coral. I've got a treat for you. You'll be going home tomorrow and I came to say 'goodbye'. You know, without all the cameras and people around."

The water is still. There is no sign of Coral. Sean looks around and notices the wet floor, and now sees that the security camera is smashed to pieces.

"Coral?!"

Startled, Sean hears a car door slam and tires squealing in the parking lot. He rushes to the gate, and sees McLavish driving away with Coral in the back of a large truck. Water sloshes from a make-shift tank as he makes his rapid getaway.

"Oh, no!" Sean exclaims, "That creep's got Coral!"

"Who's got Coral?"

Sean turns to see Surf Angel, hovering above the tank. His eyes bug out.

"Oh, great. Are you kidding me?! Kara will never let me live this down. Are you-?"

"Yes. I'm Surf Angel. Hello, Sean."

"Uh, hi," he waves, "Heard a lot about you. Kara left out how sparkly you are!"

"Thank you, Sean. Now, what's happened to Coral?"

"It's that McLavish guy! He snuck-in here, and kidnapped her! He just drove away in a big truck!"

Surf Angel nods, determined, "Alright, Sean. There's not a moment to lose! Jump on," motioning to her surfboard.

"Really?" Sean hesitates, wearily, "Are you sure it's safe?"

"It's as safe as I am sparkly!" she assures.

"Fair enough."

Surf Angel helps Sean climb onto her surfboard, and they quickly rise up into the night sky.

"Hold on, Sean." Surf Angel warns as they quickly launch forward, with lightning speed, surfing through the cloud waves.

Surf Angel strikes a determined surfer's pose while Sean lays on his stomach, clinging to the board, wind rushing through their hair.

"You can stand up now. There's no need to be afraid."

"I have a small issue with heights," he grumbles and then gasps, "Hey, look! I see them! Down there!"

Sean points down below to the truck in the

distance, which has pulled into a marina.

Surf Angel and Sean descend down the cloud wave, and land her surfboard quietly behind a snack shack.

They can see McLavish and his helpers unloading Coral onto a large watercraft idling at the dock.

"Oh, no! He's going to get away!" Sean whispers.

"Not if we splash fast!" Surf Angel remarks, "Sean, call your parents and the police."

"What are you gonna do?" Sean asks.

"I'm going to call some friends of my own."

17 - *ROCKING THE BOAT*

McLavish sits in his large overstuffed chair as his boat speeds away from the marina heading directly towards the open sea.

"If people won't give you what you want, you've just got to reach out and take it!" he laughs, "Next stop, Atlantic City!"

Suddenly out of nowhere, a thunderous splash is heard, then felt.

"What in the world is that?!" McLavish shouts.

Several more loud gigantic splashes are heard, and the boat begins to rock violently. The captain, feeling the turbulence, slows the boat as he sees a pod of Orca Whales breaching. Launching their bodies into the air, the whales crash down hard into the water. The force of their weight creates large curtains of water, rocking the boat violently from side to side.

McLavish is thrown out of his chair and tumbles onto the hard wooden deck.

Trying to regain his balance, "Why have you slowed down?!" he growls to the captain, trying to stand up, "Don't slow down!"

"The whales," the captain points, "I don't want to run into them!"

"Who cares?" he shouts, "They're just big fish!"

"Actually, sir, they're mammals," the captain corrects.

"If you don't move this boat, you'll be swimming with them! Now go!"

"You're the boss," he shrugs.

The captain reluctantly powers the boat forward. Suddenly, a strange sputtering noise is heard, and the boat begins to jerk and lurch and slows to a stop.

"I said 'go!' GO! Faster!" McLavish insists.

"I'm trying," the captain says, "It's the engine, sir.

There's something wrong with the engine."

The captain turns off the motor. He and McLavish rush below to inspect the problem. Peering down, they can see that the engine propellers are completely entangled with kelp and seaweed.

"You fix that!" McLavish points and shouts, "I'm going back to the helm!"

The captain takes out a knife and begins to cut away at the slippery kelp. Suddenly, two dolphins surface carrying a long strand of seaweed in their mouths. It's Coral's parents! Quickly, they surprise the captain and wrap the seaweed around his wrists and pull tight, making him drop the knife. They chatter and squeak in delight and then splash him for good measure.

"What the-? OW!" the captain loudly exclaims in utter disbelief.

Misunderstanding, McLavish shouts back, "NOW?"

Excited to be underway, he reaches over to turn the key in the ignition.

Stunned, he sees that the key is now gone.

"Where did it go?" McLavish asks himself.

Looking around frantically, he sees a pelican perched on his super comfy chair with the boat key dangling from his beak.

"Not **YOU** again! It can't be! That's **MY** key!" he exclaims, grabbing for it.

The pelican jumps up and jerks away from McLavish's reach.

"Alright, easy," McLavish reasons, "Steady. I won't hurt you, you miserable thief!""

With that, the pelican flutters his wings, throws his head back, and swallows the key with one large gulp.

"Why you flying rat!"

McLavish, enraged, lunges for the pelican. The pelican quickly dodges and flies into the air. McLavish tumbling forward, misjudges the yacht's ledge and careens overboard, creating a huge splash.

"Help! Agh! Man overboard!" he panics, splashing wildly and flailing his arms,

"HELP! Extremely important man overboard!"

Suddenly, a life preserver is tossed and plops on the surface right next to McLavish. Quickly he grabs it, and struggles to fit it around his ample waist.

Preserver securely in place, McLavish sighs in relief, "Thank you ever so much."

McLavish looks around for his rescuer. Startled, he sees Surf Angel hovering with the pesky pelican perched on her surfboard.

Rubbing his eyes, he remarks, "An angel that surfs? Miss Angel, did I drown?"

Surf Angel giggles, "No, you old barnacle."

A loud horn blares in the distance.

"Perfect timing." Surf Angel smiles.

"This is the Coast Guard! I repeat: This is the Coast Guard!" a loud speaker announces, cutting through the fog.

"Oh, no!" McLavish sighs, "This is most unfortunate."

Floating upwards on her surfboard, Surf Angel drifts up and away into the clouds.

McLavish watching, shouts to her, "Hey, don't go! We need to talk! I can make you famous!"

Kara, Sean, Mom and Dad are together on the deck of the Coast Guard boat.

Sean looking through borrowed binoculars, shouts, "There it is! There's McLavish's boat!"

In quick time, the Coast Guard and family pull up next to, and board the yacht. McLavish is slowly pulled up and out of the water. Dripping and sputtering, he pleads to the Coast Guard.

"Officer, please, I am innocent. I wasn't stealing the dolphin. I was rescuing her!" the soaking McLavish proclaims.

"What?" the Coast Guard asks, skeptically.

"That's right!" McLavish insists, "I was trying to save her from that crazed captain!" pointing, "He's the real culprit!"

"ME?!" the seaweed shackled captain shouts, "This was all your idea! This is your boat! I was just following your orders!"

"Ridiculous! Besides, there's no way to prove whose boat it truly is!" McLavish shrugs, "It's my word against yours!"

"Sir, the back of the boat has S.S. McLavish painted on it," the Coast Guard captain glares.

"Oh, drat," McLavish slumps, defeated.

The Coast Guard arrests and handcuffs the Captain and McLavish, and then transports the downcast pair to the Coast Guard boat.

18 - *SECRETS REVEALED*

The family surrounds Coral's water filled pen on the yacht. She is now safe and they are extremely happy to be reunited with her.

All of a sudden, a shock wave is felt, rocking the yacht from side to side. Looking around they see the boat is surrounded by phosphorescent blue plankton.

Quickly, they all grab onto the rails to keep from falling down.

"Whoa!" gasps Sean.

"Hold on!" Dad tells his family, "It must be a typhoon!"

Everyone's hair is whipped around from the force of the wind that has been created by a swarm of green and blue flying fish coning skyward.

"What is happening?" Mom breathes.

Reacting to the environmental enthusiasm, Coral begins to glow electric sparkly pink.

The family sees Coral change and watches her in awe.

Surf Angel appears and drifts down on her surfboard to the boat. She joyfully announces to the children and parents, "Coral is now ready to be reunited with the ocean and her family."

"It's an- an-" Dad stammers.

"Certainly looks like a-" Mom agrees.

"Mom, Dad, this is Surf Angel," Kara introduces, "We're friends!"

"I know it's a lot," Sean sighs, "but trust me on this one, it's best to just go with it."

Mom and Dad stare blankly and wave "Hello". Kara giggles.

Surf Angel compliments them, "Your family worked together to ensure that this special dolphin is reunited with her family pod. Your selfless efforts are an incredible example of kindness and caring. You have dedicated your lives to helping others - the greatest gift of all. Thank you from all your friends on the land and the sea."

Sean puts his arm around Kara's shoulder. Kara hugs him tightly.

"The time has come at last," Surf Angel nods.

Reassuringly and holding Coral's face close to hers, Surf Angel whispers quietly, "Your magical life is just beginning."

Surf Angel uses her powers and gently lifts Coral skyward. Then carefully she slips her into the ocean with a small neat splash.

"Off you go, little one, " Surf Angel nudges.

Now submerged in the water, the family watches in awe as Coral sends a ripple of sparkles through the surrounding water.

Standing on the deck, the human family watches as their little pink dolphin friend begins to swim.

Looking back at the boat, Coral timidly begins to stretch her pectoral fins. Tentatively, she circles the boat testing her new found strength and power.

Sensing her hesitation, Sean begins to shout words of encouragement. The children can barely contain their excitement at the sight of Coral swimming at last.

Side by side, the family watches Coral swim away, gain speed and slice through the water. Suddenly, she leaps high up into the air, waving her glowing pink tail enthusiastically.

The family shouts happily, "Yay! Coral!"

From far away, whales, seals, sea birds and Coral's dolphin family begin singing a chorus of welcome sounds that slowly fills the air.

Hearing this joyous music in the distance, Coral turns toward the sound and dives deep. She then bursts through the surface of the water, and propels high into the air one more time near the boat.

A full aerial somersault and perfect dive complete, Coral swims vigorously out to meet the expectant group.

Finally, together, the dolphin pod excitedly greets Coral in splashing waterfalls of sun-kissed water.

Nuzzling and squeaking, reunited at last, Coral greets her dolphin family, joyfully they tumble and roll together in a watery embrace.

19 - *MAGICAL REUNION*

Out on the horizon there is a shimmer of dazzling sunrise sparkles. Pink and orange clouds meet sherbet-colored water.

Surrounded by their ocean friends, Coral and her family swim out to sea in the rising sun. Their silhouetted dorsal fins slice the water as they depart jumping and diving with sheer joy.

Surf Angel observes the jubilant scene in the golden early morning light.

"It's time for me to go as well," she sighs.

Kara reaches up and hugs her, "I'll miss you, Surf Angel."

"Me too," adds Sean.

Surf Angel smiles, "Always remember to look to the night sky. Whenever you see a sparkle and shimmer, you'll know I am watching over you."

Surf Angel gently unfurls and flaps her wings, showering the family with dazzling sparkles.

Kara and her family marvel at the sight, watching in awe as billowing cumulous clouds gather in the rising sun. Surf Angel surfs from the water's surface, and flies up high into the clouds, leaving a wondrous trail of brilliant light and sparkles in her wake. In the blink of an eye, she is gone.

Kara and her family board the Coast Guard's boat. The crew stares out to the horizon in astonishment.

"Wow. What did we just witness?" the Coast Guard Captain asks everyone around him.

Mom and Dad look at him and wonder the same. Kara and Sean look at each other and smile, "Magic."

20 - *HEAVENLY HOME*

Surf Angel now back in her cloudy heavenly realm, she contentedly looks down to the Earth below and smiles.

Laying on her downy fluffy cloud, Surf Angel sends out a loving wish to all her earthly friends.

Softly, she whispers,

"Surf Your Dreams."

ABOUT THE AUTHORS

Co-Author, Terry Kraszewski

Terry grew up in sunny Southern California, soaking up the sunshine, saltwater and a love of the surfing lifestyle.

Terry has a degree in Early Childhood Development. Living near the ocean has been a wonderful place to raise two beautiful and talented daughters.

Terry owns a surf boutique called Ocean Girl in La Jolla, California, which features her own brand of surf inspired clothing called "Surf Angel."

An "anything is possible" attitude created her optimistic approach and involvement in issues ranging from protecting the environment to finding the cure for Cystic Fibrosis.

Co-Author, Heather Dawn Kraszewski

Heather was diagnosed with Cystic Fibrosis at four months of age. Living a positive life full of laughter, she inspires and teaches valuable lessons about how life should be enjoyed and treasured each and every day.

Heather has a degree in Film and Television and has worked on many television shows and feature films. She is also a gifted writer and story teller.

Having the beach as her playground, Heather has always felt a strong connection with the sea and the wonderful animals that share the ocean with her.

Illustrator, Bonnie Bright

Bonnie Bright is a full time, freelance artist, balancing her time between hard work, family and beach volleyball. Her art and animation appear on a wide range of educational computer games, children's books and children's shows. The opportunity to utilize talents that include fine arts, portrait painting, 3D and traditional background art, 2D animation and web design has Bright "Surfing Her Dreams!"

Bright's other illustrated titles include, "The Tangle Tower" (co-authored by Bright), "I Love You All the Time," "I'm In the Bathroom!" and "With Me Always."

You might also enjoy our children's bedtime story:

Surf Angel

Join the Surf Angel on her magical adventures to the ocean kingdom below, where she visits her sea life friends to prepare them for a safe night of sleep.

Included is an audio CD and delightful illustrations that will captivate children of all ages and remind us to be respectful stewards of the sea's natural treasures.

Made in the USA
Columbia, SC
06 February 2019